READING RECOVERY

MY GRANDMA, the WITCH

Written by Adrian Robert
Illustrated by Gioia Fiammenghi

Troll Associates

Library of Congress Cataloging in Publication Data

Robert, Adrian.
My grandma, the witch.

Summary: Gwen's grandmother says she's too young to be a witch, but one day Gwen finds her grandma's book of secrets and decides to try some spells.
1. Children's stories, American. [1. Witches—Fiction] I. Fiammenghi, Gioia, ill. II. Title.
PZ7.R5385My 1985 [E] 84-8742
ISBN 0-8167-0422-8 (lib. bdg.)
ISBN 0-8167-0423-6 (pbk.)

Printed in the United States of America.

10 9 8 7 6 5 4 3 2 1

MY GRANDMA, the WITCH

PRINCIPAL

My grandma's a witch.

I may as well tell you that. Everybody else does. They say, "This is Gwen. Her grandma's a witch."

My mother doesn't like that at all.

My grandma is a witch. But she won't teach *me* how to be one, not since the night I turned the spinach into toads. They jumped off the plate and hopped around the table.

One hopped into the gravy bowl. *Splash!* The gravy went all over the tablecloth.

Another toad hopped onto my sister's lap. My sister screamed. Mother dropped her coffee cup.

One hid under the ivy plant stand.

Another hopped into the kitchen and hid. We still haven't found him.

Mother was not amused.

Mother's not a witch, but she can *really* get angry. Off she marched me to Grandma's house. "I don't want Gwen doing witchy things," Mom told Grandma. "She has to learn to *eat* her spinach, not turn it into toads. *I don't want toads in my gravy bowl.*"

"Toads in the gravy," Grandma said. "Oh, dear. That *is* bad. Gravy's much too thick for toads to swim in."

Mother's face grew pale. "That's not the point. I don't want you to teach Gwen things like that. I want you to promise you won't teach her to be a witch!"

I held my breath.

Home Sweet Home

“Have some mint tea, Molly,” Grandma said. “It’s very good for the nerves.”

My mother folded her arms.

Grandma poured some tea. She stirred it

slowly and smiled at my mother. "You're right, Molly," she agreed. "Anyone who turns spinach into toads is much too young to learn witchy things."

She tried to frown at me, but Grandma is not a scary witch. "I'm ashamed of you, Gwen," she said. "*Iggety—Ziggety—Alla—Zed!* Witchy secrets, leave this girl's head!"

Sassafras, Grandma's pet cat, blinked. The candles flickered. I closed my eyes tight.

When I opened them, I couldn't remember anything about turning spinach into toads. Mother was smiling. Everybody was happy again. Except for me!

I wanted to learn how to be a witch!

In school everybody says, "Gwen's grandma's a witch. Why can't Gwen do nice witchy things? Why can't she make our homework do itself? Why can't she make our team win all the races? Why can't she turn our school lunch into pepperoni pizza?"

I wanted our homework to do itself. I wanted to win all the races. I wanted to make wishes come true the way Grandma could.

Only I didn't know how. And Grandma wouldn't teach me. It was going to be a long school year.

Luckily, I knew where the secrets were. They were kept in Grandma's green book. It had a lock on it and was kept on a high shelf. Grandma used to let me look at it in the good old days, before I turned the spinach into toads.

If I wanted to be a witch, I knew I had to read that book. I didn't say anything to Grandma. I didn't ask any more witchy questions. That night I even ate my spinach.

In school I worked hard on history and spelling. But what I really wanted to learn was in Grandma's green book.

One afternoon I went to Grandma's house after school.

To my surprise, the door was left open. The teapot was still hot. Freshly baked cookies shaped like jack-o'-lanterns sat on the kitchen table.

No one was home—not even Sassafras. Then I realized what had happened. Sassafras was out chasing another dog. And Grandma was chasing Sassafras.

I sat down to wait. I drank some tea and ate three jack-o'-lantern cookies one after another.

Suddenly someone moved behind me. "Yowww?" It was only Sassafras. He was alone. "Mrrow," he said, and rubbed against my leg.

“You’re in trouble,” I said. “Wait till Grandma finds you!”

“Mrrah,” said Sassafras. He wasn’t a bit upset. He jumped up on the kitchen table,

but there wasn't much room for him. Grandma's big bowl took up a lot of room. In it was a strange-looking mess. Sassafras sniffed it and spat.

I wondered what Grandma was making this time. There were all kinds of jars by the bowl. One was labeled *bats' teeth*. Another said *hair of newt*.

Sassafras found a dead spider. Then he found the cookie plate. "Sassafras, no!" I lifted the cookie plate so he couldn't grab a cookie.

Then I saw it. Lying underneath the cookie plate was Grandma's green book. And it was open! I couldn't believe it.

I opened the book to the first page. Finally I could learn the secrets of how to be a real witch!

But Grandma's book wasn't like the books at school. It was full of strange writing. The ink was faded. I couldn't make out the words.

I put the cookie plate inside a cupboard.

"Mrrow?" asked Sassafras. Then I tried another page in the green book. Sassafras tried to read the page, too.

"I wish you could read," I said. "I wish you could talk and tell me secrets. I wish I could remember what I used to know." Sassafras shook his head.

I turned some pages. Then I found a word I could read: Spells.

I could read the letters on this page. But I didn't know what the words meant. They were witchy words like Grandma used.

Maybe there was a spell to make me remember. Maybe there was a spell to make Sassafras talk.

It couldn't hurt to try.

I took a deep breath. I said the letters aloud.

"Zappo—Dappo—Lappa—Dee!"

Thunder crashed. A puff of smoke rose to the ceiling. Sassafras the cat wasn't there anymore! A stone statue sat there instead. It looked like Sassafras. A faint sound came from inside the statue. *"Mrrow!"* It sounded like him, too. And it was mad.

"Oh, poor Sassafras! I'm sorry!"

"*Mmmmm!!!*" said the statue. I knew what that meant: *Do something!* I looked at the next spell in the book. Maybe that would undo the first one.

"*Gikkl—Kikkl—Ikkl—Zip!*"

Whammo! Fire burst out in the fireplace. It roared up the chimney and filled the room with smoke. Sassafras was still a statue. I tried another spell.

"Chick—Tick—A—Boom!"

The cupboard door flew open. The jack-o'-lantern cookies marched out. Then they started to grow and turn into real jack-o'-lanterns!

"Mmmmm!" the statue tried to shout.

"Oh, Sassafras, what shall I do? *Alla—Walla—Wham!"*

Grandma's wooden spoon started to stir the mixing bowl. It stirred faster and faster. The mess inside the bowl splashed out.

The fireplace smoke got thicker. The jack-o'-lanterns were almost as big as I was. Their faces scared me. I wished I'd never wanted to be a witch! Everything was going crazy!

Suddenly the front door flew open.

There stood Grandma!

"*Boom—A—Tick—Chick!*" she shouted.

Whammo! The jack-o'-lanterns stopped growing. They shrank back into cookies and marched back onto their plate.

"*Zip—Ikkl—Kikkl—Gikkl!*" shouted Grandma.

The awful smoke disappeared.

"*Wham—Walla—Alla!*"

The spoon stopped stirring. The bowl stopped splashing.

Grandma looked at me. I tried not to look at her.

"*Mmmmm!*" said the statue.

Grandma turned. "Oh my, oh me," she said. She frowned at the stone Sassafras. "You are involved too, you know. You ran away. That's how Gwen found my book!"

"*Mrrow,*" said the statue. It sounded ashamed.

Grandma shook her head. "I guess you've been punished enough," she said. "*Dee—Lappa—Dappo—Zappo.*"

When the thunder and lightning cleared, the statue was gone. Sassafras jumped to the top of the cupboard and glared at me.

"I don't blame him," Grandma said. "Gwen, how could you?"

"I didn't mean to," I said. "I was just trying to learn your secrets. I was just trying to be a witch like you."

"You're too young," Grandma said. "You just want to be a witch for fun—to make mischief and to get out of things you don't want to do. That's not what being a good witch is all about."

I thought about spinach and toads.
I thought about school lunch and pizza.
I thought about what I had done to Sassafras.
I felt like I was getting smaller, just like the jack-o'-lanterns.

"I'm sorry," I said in a little voice.

"That doesn't undo anything, does it?" Grandma said. "Go home, Gwen. *I* have to undo all the mischief you let loose here."

"Can you?" I remembered the scary faces on the jack-o'-lanterns, and I started to shake.

Grandma's face grew serious. She shook her finger at me and lowered her voice.

"Come here. I'm going to tell you the most important secret of all."

I listened so hard my ears almost flapped.

"Good is always stronger than evil,"

Grandma said. "Kindness is always stronger than mischief. If you don't know that, it doesn't matter what you know. And until you know it, you can't be trusted with any secrets. Now go home, child! I have lots of work to do!"

All the way home I thought about what Grandma had said. It made sense. I had wanted to be a witch mostly for mischief. How did Grandma know that?

That was another of her secrets. Maybe someday I would know all of them. I gave a little skip. Grandma hadn't said she *wouldn't* teach me—just that she wouldn't until I was old enough!

Till then I'll leave the witchy things to Grandma. After all, I'm still pretty lucky. Not everyone has a grandma who is a good witch.

There was a nice surprise waiting for me at home. For dinner Mom had ordered a large pepperoni pizza. This might turn out to be a good year after all.